KATIE WOO
and PEDRO
Mysteries

The Birthday Party Mystery

by Fran Manushkin

illustrated by Tammie Lyon

WITHDRAWN

PICTURE WINDOW BOOKS
a capstone imprint

Published by Picture Window Books, an imprint of Capstone
1710 Roe Crest Drive, North Mankato, Minnesota 56003
capstonepub.com

Text copyright © 2022 by Fran Manushkin
Illustrations copyright © 2022 by Capstone

Library of Congress Cataloging-in-Publication Data
Names: Manushkin, Fran, author. | Lyon, Tammie, illustrator.
Title: The birthday party mystery / by Fran Manushkin ; illustrated by Tammie Lyon.
Description: North Mankato, Minnesota : Picture Window Books, an imprint of Capstone, [2022] | Series: Katie Woo and Pedro mysteries | Audience: Ages 5–7. | Audience: Grades K–1. | Summary: Katie's birthday is tomorrow, but she just cannot wait to find out what her present will be. So she and Pedro follow Katie's parents as they go shopping. None of the places they stop seem present-worthy, and Katie is disappointed. But when she gets home a big surprise is waiting for her.
Identifiers: LCCN 2021029876 (print) | LCCN 2021029877 (ebook) | ISBN 9781663958686 (hardcover) | ISBN 9781666332285 (paperback) | ISBN 9781666332292 (pdf)
Subjects: LCSH: Woo, Katie (Fictitious character)—Juvenile fiction. | Chinese Americans—Juvenile fiction. | Hispanic Americans—Juvenile fiction. | Surprise birthday parties—Juvenile fiction. | Birthdays—Juvenile fiction. | Gifts—Juvenile fiction. | CYAC: Birthdays—Fiction. | Gifts—Fiction. | Chinese Americans—Fiction. | Hispanic Americans—Fiction. | Mystery and detective stories. | LCGFT: Detective and mystery fiction. | Picture books.
Classification: LCC PZ7.M3195 Bk 2022 (print) | LCC PZ7.M3195 (ebook) | DDC 813.54 [E]—dc23
LC record available at https://lccn.loc.gov/2021029876
LC ebook record available at https://lccn.loc.gov/2021029877

Design Elements by Shutterstock: Darcraft, Magnia
Designed by Dina Her

Table of Contents

Chapter 1

What's Katie's Gift?

Katie liked to spy!

Her birthday was coming

the next day. Katie wanted

to know what gift she was

getting.

She heard her mom tell her dad, "Every year, Katie sneaks around and spoils our surprise."

Later, Katie heard her dad
whisper to her mom, "It's
time to get Katie's present."

"I'm a great detective,"
thought Katie. "I'll follow
them for clues."

Katie's mom told Katie,
"Your dad and I are going to
get new shoes. Grandma is
going to watch you."

"I'm going to start a
big jigsaw puzzle," said
Grandma. "Do you want
to help me?"

"I can't," said Katie.
"I'm going on a bike ride
with Pedro." Maybe he
could help Katie solve the
mystery of her present!

"Don't forget to wear your helmet!" said Katie's dad.

"I promise," said Katie.

"See you later," said her parents.

Chapter 2

On the Case

When her parents drove

off, Katie jumped on her bike.

As she passed Pedro's house,

he began riding along.

Katie told him, "We are

going to solve my birthday

mystery."

The car stopped at
a farmers market. Katie
wondered, "Am I getting
veggies for my birthday?"

No! Her mom bought a
bag of cherries. Her mom
and dad began eating them.

"Nope!" said Katie. "That
is not a clue."

Katie's parents drove

away again. Then they

stopped at a hardware store.

"There could be lots of

clues at a hardware store,"

said Katie. "I hope I'm not

getting a hammer and nails

for my birthday!"

No! Her dad came out
with a rake and grass seed.

"Mom and Dad do all the
planting," said Katie. "So
that is not for me."

Then her parents headed
home.

"Something's wrong!" said
Katie. "They were supposed
to buy my present."

Chapter 3

Mystery Solved!

Katie felt sad.

"I love mysteries. But

I don't like this one!" She

walked slowly into her house.

All the lights were on!

And all her friends were

there!

"SURPRISE!" they yelled.

"HAPPY BIRTHDAY!"

"Wow!" yelled Katie. "This is terrific! But my birthday isn't today. It's tomorrow."

"We know," said her dad.

"But you are such a good spy!

The only way to surprise you

is with a day-before-your-

birthday party."

Her mom said, "We knew you were spying and would follow our car. That gave Grandma time to prepare your party."

The party was great!
They played games and
watched funny movies.
And Katie's gift was
perfect: a spy kit!

About the Author

Fran Manushkin is the author of Katie Woo, the highly acclaimed fan-favorite early-reader series, as well as the popular Pedro series. Her other books include *Happy in Our Skin*, *Plenty of Hugs!*, *Baby, Come Out!*, and the best-selling board books *Big Girl Panties* and *Big Boy Underpants*. There is a real Katie Woo: Fran's great-niece, but she doesn't get into as much trouble as the Katie in the books. Fran lives in New York City, three blocks from Central Park, where she can often be found bird-watching and daydreaming. She writes at her dining room table, without the help of her naughty cats, Goldy and Chaim.

About the Illustrator

Tammie Lyon, the illustrator of the Katie Woo and Pedro series, says that these characters are two of her favorites. Tammie has illustrated work for Disney, Scholastic, Simon and Schuster, Penguin, HarperCollins, and Amazon Publishing, to name a few. She is also an author/illustrator of her own stories. Her first picture book, *Olive and Snowflake*, was released to starred reviews from *Kirkus* and *School Library Journal*. Tammie lives in Cincinnati, Ohio, with her husband Lee and two dogs, Amos and Artie. She spends her days working in her home studio in the woods, surrounded by wildlife and, of course, two mostly-always-sleeping dogs.

Glossary

clue (KLOO)—something that helps someone find something or solve a mystery

detective (dee-TEK-tiv)—a person who works to solve mysteries

farmers market (FAR-mers MAR-kit)—a shopping area where people sell the items they grow

hardware store (HAHRD-wair STOR)—a store that sells tools and other items for homes and gardens

mystery (MISS-tur-ee)—a puzzle or crime that needs to be solved

solve (SOLV)—to find the answer to a problem

spy (SPYE)—to secretly watch and listen

All About Mysteries

A mystery is a story where the main characters must figure out a puzzle or solve a crime. Let's think about *The Birthday Party Mystery*.

Plot

In a mystery, the plot focuses on solving a problem. What is the problem in this story? Is it a real problem?

Clues

To solve a mystery, readers should look for clues. What are some of the clues in this mystery?

Red Herrings

Red herrings are bad clues. They do not help solve the mystery. Sometimes they even make the mystery harder to solve. What clues in this story were red herrings?

Thinking About the Story

1. Was the mystery in this story important to solve? Why or why not?

2. How would the story have been different if Katie stayed home, instead of following her parents? What things may have happened?

3. Did Katie and Pedro solve the mystery in this story? Explain your answer.

4. Imagine Katie really did get a rake and grass seed for her birthday gift. How do you think she would have felt?

Investigate Fingerprints

Spies and detectives sometimes collect fingerprints to help them solve a mystery. Have you ever taken a close look at fingerprints? Every person's swirly patterns in their prints are unique to just them. No two fingerprints are alike! With this activity you can compare prints from your friends and family with your own.

What you need:

- a few pieces of plain white paper

- a lead pencil

- clear sticky tape

- a magnifying glass

What you do:

1. Use the pencil to scribble out a square-shaped shading on the paper.

2. Place your thumb on the paper. Then press your thumb on the sticky side of a small piece of tape.

3. Peel off the tape and stick it on a piece of paper. This is your thumb print. Label it with your name.

4. Repeat steps 2 and 3 with friends or family members. Then use the magnifying glass to take a closer look at each print. Notice the differences among them!

Solve more mysteries with Katie and Pedro!

KATIE WOO and PEDRO Mysteries

The Mystery of the Snow Puppy

by Fran Manushkin • illustrated by Tammie Lyon

KATIE WOO and PEDRO Mysteries

The Mystery of the Stinky, Spooky Night

by Fran Manushkin • illustrated by Tammie Lyon

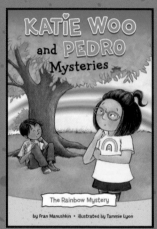

KATIE WOO and PEDRO Mysteries

The Rainbow Mystery

by Fran Manushkin • illustrated by Tammie Lyon